MR. TALL

by Roger Harg

Mr Tall was very very **very tall**.

Quite the tallest person **you've** ever met.

In fact, quite the **tallest person** you've never met, because you've **never met** anybody with legs as long as Mr Tall's **legs**.

Have you?

Now, the problem with being as tall as Mr Tall, meant that life was just one long problem.

As you can see!

"Oh dear," he used to sigh.

"Oh dear me! I do so wish that my legs weren't quite so very very very long."

He decided to go for a walk to think over his problem.

He was just stepping over a tree when he heard a voice.

A little voice.

"Hello!"

It was Mr Small, standing underneath a daisy.

But Mr Tall was so tall he couldn't see him.

So Mr Small shouted at the top of his voice.

"Hello!"

A Mr Small shout is about as loud as a bee's sneeze.

So, it took quite some time for Mr Tall to spot him.

"Oh," he said gloomily. "It's you."

"You don't look very happy," said Mr Small. "What's up?"

"I am," replied Mr Tall. "Because of these silly long legs of mine."

"Oh," said Mr Small.

Mr Small decided to cheer him up.

"Let's go for a walk together," he suggested.

So they did, which of course didn't work.

It was like a giraffe going for a walk with a mouse!

Then Mr Small had an idea.

Which did work!

And, because of the length of Mr Tall's legs, they very quickly walked all the way to the seaside.

"Come for a swim," cried Mr Small.

"Can't," replied Mr Tall. "By the time it gets deep enough for me to swim I'll be out the other side."

So Mr Small went for a swim, while Mr Tall sat down with a face which was nearly as long as his legs.

Mr Tickle came along.

"Hello," he said. "You look as if you need cheering up. Care for a tickle?"

"No thanks," replied Mr Tall. "What I would care for are some different legs. Mine are much too long."

"So are my arms," said Mr Tickle cheerfully. "But all the better for tickling!"

And off he went, chuckling, looking for somebody to tickle.

Looking for anybody to tickle!

Mr Nosey came along.

"Cheer up," he said. "You look very down in the mouth. What's the problem?"

"It's my legs," replied Mr Tall. "They're too long!"

"So's my nose," replied Mr Nosey, laughing. "But all the better for poking into other people's business!"

And he went off, looking for something to be nosey about.

Looking for anything to be nosey about.

Mr Greedy came along.

"Hello," he cried. "You look gloomy! What's wrong?"

"It's my legs," explained Mr Tall. "They're too big!"

"So is my tummy," replied Mr Greedy. "But all the better for filling with food!"

And off he went, licking his lips.

Mr Tall sat there and thought about Mr Tickle's arms, and Mr Nosey's nose, and Mr Greedy's tummy.

He smiled.

And then, he grinned.

And then he laughed out loud.

He looked at his legs, those very very very long legs of his.

"All the better for walking," he chuckled.

And walked home.

In four minutes.

Forty miles!

Mr Small came out of the sea after his short swim.

"And how am I going to get home?" he asked himself.

So, he set off walking.

All the way home.

Forty miles!

That was last year.

He got home yesterday!

3 Great Offers for MR. MEN Fans!

MR. MEN TOKEN

1 New Mr. Men or Little Miss Library Bus Presentation Cases

A brand new stronger, roomier school bus library box, with sturdy carrying handle and stay-closed fasteners.

The full colour, wipe-clean boxes make a great home for your full collection.

They're just £5.99 inc P&P and free bookmark!

☐ MR. MEN ☐ LITTLE MISS (please tick and order overleaf)

2 Door Hangers and Posters

In every Mr. Men and Little Miss book like this one, you will find a special token. Collect 6 tokens and we will send you a brilliant Mr. Men or Little Miss poster and a Mr. Men or Little Miss double sided full colour bedroom door hanger of your choice. Simply tick your choice in the list and tape a 50p coin for your two items to this page.

PLEASE STICK YOUR 50P COIN HERE

Door Hangers (please tick)
☐ Mr. Nosey & Mr. Muddle
☐ Mr. Slow & Mr. Busy
☐ Mr. Messy & Mr. Quiet
☐ Mr. Perfect & Mr. Forgetful
☐ Little Miss Fun & Little Miss Late
☐ Little Miss Helpful & Little Miss Tidy
☐ Little Miss Busy & Little Miss Brainy
☐ Little Miss Star & Little Miss Fun

Posters (please tick)
☐ MR. MEN
☐ LITTLE MISS

CUT ALONG DOTTED LINE AND RETURN THIS WHOLE PAGE

3 Sixteen Beautiful Fridge Magnets – any 2 for £2.00!
inc.P&P

They're very special collector's items!
Simply tick your first and second* choices from the list below
of any 2 characters!

1st Choice
- ☐ Mr. Happy
- ☐ Mr. Lazy
- ☐ Mr. Topsy-Turvy
- ☐ Mr. Bounce
- ☐ Mr. Bump
- ☐ Mr. Small
- ☐ Mr. Snow
- ☐ Mr. Wrong

- ☐ Mr. Daydream
- ☐ Mr. Tickle
- ☐ Mr. Greedy
- ☐ Mr. Funny
- ☐ Little Miss Giggles
- ☐ Little Miss Splendid
- ☐ Little Miss Naughty
- ☐ Little Miss Sunshine

2nd Choice
- ☐ Mr. Happy
- ☐ Mr. Lazy
- ☐ Mr. Topsy-Turvy
- ☐ Mr. Bounce
- ☐ Mr. Bump
- ☐ Mr. Small
- ☐ Mr. Snow
- ☐ Mr. Wrong

- ☐ Mr. Daydream
- ☐ Mr. Tickle
- ☐ Mr. Greedy
- ☐ Mr. Funny
- ☐ Little Miss Giggles
- ☐ Little Miss Splendid
- ☐ Little Miss Naughty
- ☐ Little Miss Sunshine

*Only in case your first choice is out of stock.

--- TO BE COMPLETED BY AN ADULT ---

To apply for any of these great offers, ask an adult to complete the coupon below and send it with the appropriate payment and tokens, if needed, to MR. MEN CLASSIC OFFER, PO BOX 715, HORSHAM RH12 5WG

☐ Please send _____ Mr. Men Library case(s) and/or _____ Little Miss Library case(s) at £5.99 each inc P&P

☐ Please send a poster and door hanger as selected overleaf. I enclose six tokens plus a 50p coin for P&P

☐ Please send me _____ pair(s) of Mr. Men/Little Miss fridge magnets, as selected above at £2.00 inc P&P

Fan's Name _____

Address _____

_____ **Postcode** _____

Date of Birth _____

Name of Parent/Guardian _____

Total amount enclosed £ _____

☐ **I enclose a cheque/postal order payable to Egmont Books Limited**

☐ **Please charge my MasterCard/Visa/Amex/Switch or Delta account** (delete as appropriate)

Card Number

Expiry date ___/___ **Signature** _____

Please allow 28 days for delivery. Offer is only available while stocks last. We reserve the right to change the terms of this offer at any time and we offer a 14 day money back guarantee. This does not affect your statutory rights. Data Protection Act: If you do not wish to receive other similar offers from us or companies we recommend, please tick this box ☐. Offers apply to UK only.

MR.MEN   LITTLE MISS
Mr. Men and Little Miss™ & ©Mrs. Roger Hargreaves

CUT ALONG DOTTED LINE AND RETURN THIS WHOLE PAGE